LAKE CLASSICS

Great American Short Stories III

Edna
FERBER

Stories retold by C.D. Buchanan
Illustrated by James Balkovek

LAKE EDUCATION
Belmont, California

LAKE CLASSICS

Great American Short Stories I

Washington Irving, Nathaniel Hawthorne, Mark Twain, Bret Harte, Edgar Allan Poe, Kate Chopin, Willa Cather, Sarah Orne Jewett, Sherwood Anderson, Charles W. Chesnutt

Great American Short Stories II

Herman Melville, Stephen Crane, Ambrose Bierce, Jack London, Edith Wharton, Charlotte Perkins Gilman, Frank R. Stockton, Hamlin Garland, O. Henry, Richard Harding Davis

Great American Short Stories III

Thomas Bailey Aldrich, Irvin S. Cobb, Rebecca Harding Davis, Theodore Dreiser, Alice Dunbar-Nelson, Edna Ferber, Mary Wilkins Freeman, Henry James, Ring Lardner, Wilbur Daniel Steele

Great British and Irish Short Stories

Arthur Conan Doyle, Saki (H. H. Munro), Rudyard Kipling, Katherine Mansfield, Thomas Hardy, E. M. Forster, Robert Louis Stevenson, H. G. Wells, John Galsworthy, James Joyce

Great Short Stories from Around the World

Guy de Maupassant, Anton Chekhov, Leo Tolstoy, Selma Lagerlöf, Alphonse Daudet, Mori Ogwai, Leopoldo Alas, Rabindranath Tagore, Fyodor Dostoevsky, Honoré de Balzac

Cover and Text Designer: Diann Abbott

Library of Congress Catalog Number: 95-76750
ISBN 1-56103-068-6
Printed in the United States of America
1 9 8 7 6 5 4 3 2 1

CONTENTS

Introduction 5

About the Author 7

Representing T.A. Buck 9

The Three of Them 27

Shore Leave 43

Thinking About the Stories 78

❦ Lake Classic Short Stories ❧

> *"The universe is made of stories, not atoms."*
> —Muriel Rukeyser

> *"The story's about you."*
> —Horace

Everyone loves a good story. It is hard to think of a friendlier introduction to classic literature. For one thing, short stories are *short*—quick to get into and easy to finish. Of all the literary forms, the short story is the least intimidating and the most approachable.

Great literature is an important part of our human heritage. In the belief that this heritage belongs to everyone, *Lake Classic Short Stories* are adapted for today's readers. Lengthy sentences and paragraphs are shortened. Archaic words are replaced. Modern punctuation and spellings are used. Many of the longer stories are abridged. In all the stories, painstaking care has been taken to preserve the author's unique voice.

Lake Classic Short Stories have something for everyone. The hundreds of stories in the collection cover a broad terrain of themes, story types, and styles. Literary merit was a deciding factor in story selection. But no story was included unless it was as enjoyable as it was instructive. And special priority was given to stories that shine light on the human condition.

Each book in the *Lake Classic Short Stories* is devoted to the work of a single author. Little-known stories of merit are included with famous old favorites. Taken as a whole, the collected authors and stories make up a rich and diverse sampler of the story-teller's art.

Lake Classic Short Stories guarantee a great reading experience. Readers who look for common interests, concerns, and experiences are sure to find them. Readers who bring their own gifts of perception and appreciation to the stories will be doubly rewarded.

🌿 Edna Ferber 🌿
(1887–1968)

About the Author

As a girl in Appleton, Wisconsin, Edna Ferber wanted to be an actress rather than a writer. But when her father became blind, 17-year-old Edna had to get a job. She quickly found work as a reporter on Appleton's newspaper, the *Daily Crescent*.

Seeing her talent, her editor at the newspaper encouraged her to keep writing. But Edna was not happy with her first story. She threw the whole book away. Her mother pulled it from the garbage and sent it to a publisher. In 1921, it came out as Ferber's first novel, *Dawn O'Hara*.

In 1924, the novel *So Big* made Ferber a best-selling author. It also earned her a Pulitzer Prize. There were more bestsellers to follow. Her novels *Show Boat*, *Cimarron*, and *Giant* became hit motion pictures, along with many another of her books. *Show Boat* also had a long run as a musical on Broadway. Ferber wrote stage plays, too, teaming up with playwright George S. Kaufman.

Ferber's tales take place in many settings. *Cimarron* tells about the 1889 land rush in Oklahoma. *American Beauty* describes the lives of Polish immigrants in Connecticut. *Come and Get It* is about the logging business in Wisconsin. *Giant* takes readers to Texas and *Ice Palace* to Alaska.

Perhaps Ferber's early interest in the theater led her to write stories that were ideal for the stage and screen. Her work was once described as "written ready-made for the movies, lacking nothing but the Technicolor."

As you read, try to imagine these stories on the big screen.

Representing
T. A. Buck

A traveling saleswoman's
life has never been easy.
Especially 80 years ago. In
this charming story you will
meet the unforgettable
Emma McChesney. Read on
for some insights into the
mind and heart of a hard-
charging career woman.

THE BEAUTY OF THE MUSIC BROUGHT HOT TEARS TO
EMMA'S EYES.

Representing T. A. Buck

Emma McChesney swung off the 2:15 train and ran for the hotel bus. To get inside, the trim, good-looking young woman had to climb over four feet. Two belonged to a fat man in brown. The other two belonged to a lean man in black. She knew why they were hogging the end seats. If they got off first at the hotel, they would get first choice of the best rooms available.

The bus smelled of mold and tobacco. Emma McChesney had spent nine years on the road. She was what people called a "drummer." As a traveling salesperson, it was her job to drum up business. She was used to the smell of buses.

Emma glanced at the fat traveling man. He was a picture in brown. He wore a brown suit, brown shoes, brown scarf, and a brown hat. Peeping over the edge of his pocket was a handkerchief with a brown border. He looked like a giant chocolate fudge.

"I'll bet he sells coffins and other undertakers' supplies," thought Emma. "And the other one—the tall, lanky one in black—I suppose his line would be sheet music. Or maybe it's phonographs. Or perhaps he's going to give a talk for the Young Men's Sunday Evening Club."

Emma's product line was ladies' underwear. She worked for T.A. Buck's Featherloom Skirt Company. During her years on the road, she had picked up a thing or two on human nature. She was not surprised to see the fat man and the thin man leap out of the bus. They were into the hotel before she had time to straighten her hat. By the time she reached the desk, the two had registered.

They were already walking upstairs behind a bellboy.

The clerk behind the desk looked blankly at Emma. Taking his time, he read her signature upside down. He looked at her without interest. Then he yelled, "Front! Show the lady up to room number 19."

A bellboy walked over and picked up Emma's bags. He headed for the stairway. Emma took three steps behind him, but then she stopped.

"Wait a minute, young man," she said. She walked back to the desk and eyed the clerk.

"You've made a mistake, haven't you?" she asked sweetly.

"Mistake?" The clerk said, staring. "Guess not."

"Oh? Think it over," drawled Emma. "I've never seen room 19, but I can describe it with both eyes shut. It's an inside room, isn't it? It's over the kitchen? It's next to the boiler room, and there's a pet rat that lives in the wall between rooms 18 and 19. And the housekeeper's room is across the hall. She coughs all night. I'm wise to the kind of welcome you fellows hand out to us women on the road. This is new territory for me—my first trip West. Think it over. Doesn't—um—room 65 strike you as being nearer my size?"

The clerk stared at Emma McChesney. Emma coolly stared back at him.

"Our aim," he began, grandly, "is to make our guests comfortable. But the last lady drummer who—"

"That's all right," interrupted Emma McChesney. "But I'm not the kind that steals towels. Most women drummers are living up to their reputations—but some of us are living 'em down. You haven't got my number, that's all."

A gleam of respect shone in the clerk's eye. He turned and pulled another key from the pigeonholes behind him.

"You win," he said. He leaned over the desk and lowered his voice. "Say, sweetie, why don't you go on into the cafe. Have a drink on me."

"Never use the stuff," answered Emma

McChesney. "Bad for the complexion. But thanks just the same. Nice little hotel you've got here."

In the hall leading to room 65, there was a great litter of pails and mops. Damp rags lay about. A vacuum cleaner was roaring in one of the rooms.

"Spring house-cleaning," explained the bellboy. He hopped over a pail.

Emma McChesney picked her way over a heap of dustcloths and a ladder.

"House-cleaning," she repeated dreamily. "Spring house-cleaning." A troubled, yearning light came into her eyes. It lingered there after the bellboy closed the door after her.

Emma McChesney took in the room in a glance. Iron bed—tan wallpaper—red carpet—stuffy smell—fly buzzing at window—sun beating in.

"Lordy, I hate to think what nineteen must be," she said to herself. She opened her bag. Out came brush, comb, tooth-brush, makeup, face cream. Quickly Emma removed the dust and dirt of travel. Then she glanced at her watch and hurried downstairs.

"Well, who knows?" she mused. "That thin guy may not work for a music house. Maybe *his* line is skirts, too. You never can tell. Anyway, I'll beat him to it."

Saturday afternoon and spring in a small, Midwestern town! Main Street was all a-bustle. Farmers' wagons came and went. A new five-and-ten-cent store was having its grand opening. All 32 of the town's automobiles were dashing up and down the street. A crowd waited for the next streetcar.

Emma McChesney found herself strolling when she should have been hustling. She was on her way to the Novelty Cloak and Suit Store. But she was aware of a vague, strangely restless feeling in the region of her heart. Or was it her liver? Or maybe her lungs?

She went into the store and asked for the buyer. Emma was a fine saleswoman. She landed a big order on the spot. For a woman of her skills, it didn't matter that the store was full of customers.

As she was leaving, the store owner

looked approvingly at the trim young saleswoman. He reached for his hat. "You're new in town," he said. "Let's go and have—ah—a little something. Since you're a lady, it will be on me."

"No thanks," Emma said wearily.

On her way back to the hotel, she took her time. She looked in the shop windows and watched the shoppers hurrying by. She looked different from the other women she saw.

Maybe it was her big city hat. Maybe it was the high style of her shoes. But it was clear to her and to everyone that she didn't live in this town. Most of the women were busy buying food for their Sunday dinners. That vaguely restless feeling seized her again.

There were rows of plump chickens in the butcher-shop windows, and big juicy roasts. New vegetables glowed behind the grocers' plate glass. She saw tender green lettuces and coral tomatoes. There were bins of peas and string beans.

Suddenly a wild longing came over the businesslike soul of Emma McChesney.

She wanted to go into the butcher's shop and select a ten-pound roast. She wanted to poke her fingers into the ribs of a chicken. She wanted to order sweet potatoes and soup-bones, and apples for pies. Suddenly she ached to put on an apron and roll out noodles.

Emma was still fighting these wild feelings as she walked back to the hotel. She went up to her stuffy room and sat on the edge of the bed. She stared long and hard at the faded tan wallpaper.

There's just something about tan wallpaper. If you stare at it long enough, you can begin to see things. Emma McChesney, who made good money selling Featherloom petticoats, saw this:

A kitchen. It was full of mixing bowls and saucepans. From the oven came spluttering and hissing sounds. There was the scent of freshly baked cookies.

Emma McChesney saw herself in there, wearing an apron. Her sleeves were rolled up. Her hair was somewhat wild. One lock was white where she had pushed it back with a floury hand. Her cheeks were pink and her eyes very bright. She was trimming dough from the edges of pie tins. There were things on top of the stove that demanded tasting and stirring. A neighbor came in to borrow a cup of molasses. . . .

Then a buzzing fly landed on Emma McChesney's left eyebrow. She swatted at it, and the picture in her mind disappeared. Slowly she stood up.

"Drat!" she said, wearily. She tucked in her blouse and went down to supper.

The dining room was very warm. A waitress filled Emma's glass with ice water. "I'm dying for something cool, and green, and fresh," Emma remarked. "Something springish and tempting."

"Well, we have ham and eggs, mutton chops, cold ham, cold roast—"

"Just two fried eggs then," Emma said hopelessly. "And some tea."

After supper she passed through the lobby. The place was filled with men. Some were sitting in the big leather chairs at the window. Some stood about, smoking and talking. The whole scene looked very bright, and cheery, and sociable. Emma turned to climb the stairs to her room. She felt that she, too, would like to sit in one of the big leather chairs and talk to someone.

Someone was playing the piano in the parlor. She glanced in through the open doors. Then she stopped.

A fat man in a crumpled suit was seated at the piano, playing. His hat was pushed back on his head and a big cigar was in his mouth. He was playing Mendelssohn's *Spring Song*. Not as it is often played by sweet young girls. Under his fingers, it was a trembling, laughing, sobbing thing. He was playing it in a way that made you stare straight ahead and swallow hard.

Emma McChesney leaned her head against the door. The man at the piano did not turn. So she tiptoed in and slipped into a chair. She sat very still. As she listened, the past-that-might-have-been and the future-that-was-to-be stretched behind and before her. Strangely this is often the case when we listen to beautiful music.

Now she stared ahead with eyes that were very wide open and bright. The beauty of the music brought on a hot haze of tears. She shut her eyes and wept quietly and heart-brokenly. The tears slid down her cheeks and dropped on her silk blouse. But she didn't care a bit.

Then the last lovely note died away. The piano player's hands dropped limply to his sides. Emma McChesney stared at them. They were slim, sensitive hands, tapering and delicate. As Emma stared, the man turned slowly on the stool. His plump, pink face was sad.

He watched Emma McChesney as she sat up and dried her eyes. A satisfied light dawned in his face.

"Thanks," he said. He mopped his face with a brown-edged handkerchief.

"You—you can't be the famous pianist, Paderewski. He's thin. But if he plays any better than that, I don't want to hear him. You've upset me for the rest of the week. You've started me thinking about things that—that—"

The fat pianist leaned forward. His thin hands were tightly clasped.

"About things that you're trying to forget," he said. "It starts me that way, too. That's why I don't touch the keys for weeks sometimes. Say, what do you think of a man who can play like that—and who is out on the road for a living? Just because it's a sure thing.

"Music! That's my gift. And I've buried it. Why, I'd rather play the piano in a five-cent moving picture house than do what I'm doing now. But my old man wanted his son to be a businessman. I was darn fool enough to think he was right. Why can't people do the things they're meant to do! Not one person in a thousand does. Why, take you! I don't know you from Eve, of course. But from the way you cried, I know you're busy regretting."

"Regretting?" Emma wailed loudly. "Do you know what I am? I'm a lady drummer. And do you know what I want to do this minute? I want to clean house. I want to slosh around with a pail of hot, soapy water! That's what I want to do."

"Well, why don't you go on and do it then," said the fat man.

"Do it? I haven't any house to clean. I got my divorce ten years ago, and I've been on the road ever since. I don't know why I stick. I get a good, fat salary and commissions. But it's no life for a woman. I know it, but I can't figure out how to quit. It's different for a man on the road. He can spend his evenings going to shows. Or he can play some cards. Do you know what I do?"

"No," answered the fat man. "What?"

"Evenings, I go to my room and sew or read. *Sew!* Every button on my clothes is moored so tight you can't tear 'em off. When I find a hole in my stockings, I'm thrilled! It's something to mend. And read? Everything from the rules of the house to the *Swell Set* magazine.

"It's getting on my nerves. And on Sunday mornings, I go to church. I get green with envy watching the other women there. You can tell by the look on their faces that company's coming for dinner. They're wondering if the hired girl has basted the chicken often enough. Or if she remembered to put the celery in cold water—"

The fat man banged one fist down on the piano keys.

"I'm through," he said. "I quit tonight! I've got my own life to live. Here, will you shake on it? I'll quit if you will. You're a born housekeeper. You don't belong on the road any more than I do. It's now or never. When I get to the Pearly Gates, I'm going to be ready for Saint Peter. He'll ask me, you know, what I've done with my talents."

"Oh, you're right!" Emma sobbed.

"By the way," interrupted the fat man, "what's your line?"

"Petticoats. I represent T.A. Buck's Featherloom Skirts. What's yours?"

"Suffering cats!" shouted the fat man. "Are you the one who took that big order from Novelty Cloak and Suit today? You spoiled a sale for me!"

"You! Are you—"

"You bet I am. I sell a great little underskirt.The Strauss's Sans-silk

Petticoat! Warranted not to crack, rip, or fall into holes. Greatest little underskirt in the whole country."

Emma McChesney straightened her collar and sat up with a jerk.

"Oh, now, don't give me that bunk," she said. "You've got a good little seller, all right. But that guarantee doesn't hold water. I know that stuff. Two days after you wear it, it's as limp as a rag. It's showy, all right—but if you take a line like mine, why—"

"My customers swear by me," the man said. "I go to DeKalb tomorrow. There's Nussbaum, of the Paris Emporium, the biggest store there. He just—"

"*I* go to DeKalb, too," Emma remarked. The light of battle was in her eye.

"You mean," the fat man gently reminded her, "that you *were* going to DeKalb. But that's all over now."

"Huh?" said Emma.

"Our agreement, you know. You aren't going back on that. It's the cottage and Sunday dinner for you—remember?"

"Of course," agreed Emma sweetly. "I

think I'll go up to bed now. Didn't get much sleep last night on the train."

"Won't you—er—come down and have a little something to drink?" said the fat man. "Or we could have it sent up here."

"You're the third man that's asked me that today," snapped Emma McChesney.

"No offense," the fat man said quickly. "I just thought it would bind our bargain. Guess I'll go down and get a smoke now."

Down in the lobby the fat man was talking to the clerk.

"I want to leave a call for 6:30," he was saying. "Not a minute later. I've got to get on that 7:35 train for DeKalb. Got a Sunday customer there."

As he turned away, the telephone rang at the desk. The clerk answered.

"Clerk. Yes, ma'am. No, ma'am, there's no train out of here tonight for DeKalb. Tomorrow morning at 7:35. I sure will. Wake you at 6:30? You can count on it."

The Three of Them

Everyone suffers when a nation's boys go off to war. This touching story is set during World War I. It's a heartbreaking time for every soldier's mother— even if she's a Broadway star. But how can a hotel housekeeper be of any comfort to the great Geisha McCoy?

"I CAN'T HOLD THE AUDIENCE ANYMORE. THE HARDER I WORK, THE COLDER THEY GET."

The Three
of Them

For 11 years Mrs. Martha Foote had been head housekeeper at the Senate Hotel, Chicago. Unseen and unknown, she had catered to that great mass known as the Traveling Public. Her carpets had known the tread of kings, and show girls, and buyers from Montana. Her sheets had soothed the tired limbs of presidents, and princesses, and prima donnas. For the Senate Hotel is more than a hotel. It is a Chicago institution. The whole world comes through its revolving front door.

For 11 years Martha Foote had seen

people throwing their grimy suitcases on her white bedspreads. They wiped their muddy boots on her bath towels. They scratched their matches on her wallpaper. Spilled their greasy crumbs on her carpet. Walked off with her dresser scarves and pincushions.

Eleven years of hotel housekeeping provide a deep knowledge of human nature. It includes things that no living being *ought* to know about other people. All told, this experience had turned Martha Foote into a very patient, understanding woman. Anyone at the Senate Hotel would certainly say so. Martha Foote's serene, kind nature was admired by all.

In the quiet of her room, the housekeeper of the Senate Hotel opened her eyes this Tuesday morning. It was 6:30 A.M. "It can't be as bad as yesterday. It *can't*," she assured herself.

Yesterday had been thick, murky, oozy with trouble. Two conventions, three banquets. The lobby was so full of soldiers in khaki that it looked like a sandstorm. There was a strike in the laundry. So there was a shortage of towels. And through it all came the constant, nagging complaints of the dragon in room 618.

Yes, 618 had arrived on Monday morning. By Monday night every telephone operator had the nervous jumps. The woman had changed her room, and then changed back again. She had quarreled with the room clerk. She had complained about the service, the food, the linen, and the noise. She complained about the color of the furniture. She said she couldn't live with that color. It made her sick.

Between 8:30 and 10:30 that night there was a lull. Six-eighteen was doing her show at the Majestic Theater. For the woman in room 618 was Geisha McCoy— one of the most famous entertainers of her day. For singing a few simple songs, Geisha McCoy got thousands of dollars a night. Her songs were warm and sweet and human. They made people laugh and they made people cry. Her audiences loved her, and they told her so—until very recently.

The past six months had changed Geisha McCoy. She still sang her songs every day. They were still human songs about everyday, human people. But now her songs sounded lifeless. Now her fans were saying, "You should have heard her five years ago. I guess she's about through now."

On Tuesday morning, the telephone jangled. You might say it tore through Martha Foote's half-wakened senses. "Something tells me not to answer," she thought to herself.

"Yes?"

"Mrs. Foote? This is Healy, the night clerk. Mrs. Foote, I think you'd better step down to 618 and see what's wrong. She sick, or something. Hysterics. Complaining about a noise. She says if we don't stop it right away—"

"I'll go down. What kind of noise?"

"She kept talking about a wail—a kind of groaning. And she said there were dull raps on the wall, behind the bed."

Ten minutes later, Martha Foote was standing at the door of 618. She was dressed for work. Taking a deep breath, she knocked.

"Come in!"

The woman was in bed. Her hair was pushed back wildly. Her arms were clasped about her knees. The room was in total disorder. Trays of dishes. Books and magazines. Cigarette stubs. The ceiling lights, the wall lights, and the light from two lamps beat down.

The white-faced woman in the bed stared, hollow eyed, at Martha Foote. From the door, Martha Foote gazed serenely back. A small smile crept into Geisha McCoy's face. She said, "I wouldn't have believed it."

"Believed what?" inquired Martha Foote, pleasantly.

"That there was anybody left in the world like you. Imagine looking like that at 6:30 A.M.! Is that all your own hair?"

"Absolutely."

"Some people have all the luck."

Martha Foote stepped farther into the

room and closed the door behind her.

"Listen!" the tired-looking woman in the bed said in a whisper. "What's that?"

From the wall behind the bed came a low, weird sound. It was half-wail, half-croaking moan. A clanking, then, as of chains. A *s-s-swish*. Then three dull raps—seemingly from the wall itself.

Relief flooded over Martha Foote. A smile played over her lips. But Geisha McCoy was furious.

"Look here! You may think this is all quite funny, but—"

"I don't. I *don't*. Wait a minute." Martha Foote turned and was gone. An instant later the weird sounds stopped. Martha Foote was back at the door, smiling. She brought forward the small figure of Anna Czarnik, sixth-floor scrubwoman. She was dressed in blue calico. The toes of her shoes were curled up from so much scrubbing on her knees.

"This is Mrs. Anna Czarnik, of Poland," Martha said. "She is the source of the blood-curdling moan. Also the swishing, and the clanking, and the rapping. There is a service stairway just on the other side of this wall. Anna Czarnik was scrubbing it. Wet rag swishing. Pail clanking. That was her scrub brush striking the stair corner with dull raps."

"You're forgetting the wail," Geisha McCoy said. Her voice was as cold as ice.

"No, I'm not. She says she was singing a Polish folk-song. It's called a—what was that, Anna?"

"*Dumka.*"

"It's called a *dumka*. It's a song of mourning, you see. Of grief. And of bitterness against the enemies who have invaded her country."

Geisha McCoy fell back onto the pillows. "What kind of hotel is this, anyway?" she asked. "People wailing away, behind the wall."

"I'm sorry. You can go now, Anna. No more singing, remember!"

Anna Czarnik nodded and left.

"You have no business allowing things like that, you know," said Geisha McCoy. "One word from me at the office, and that woman would lose her job."

"Don't say it, then," interrupted Martha Foote. She came over to the bed. Her quick fingers began to straighten the tumbled covers. She removed a jumble of magazines. She flicked away the crumbs. "I'm sorry you were disturbed. Of course, you're right. She shouldn't have been singing so loudly."

"What about me?" cried Geisha McCoy. "I've had no sleep and I go on stage at four! And I'm sick, I tell you! Sick!"

Then she flung herself, face down, on the pillow. She began to sob.

That helped Martha Foote make up her mind. She flicked off the glaring ceiling lights and sat down beside the shaken woman. She laid a cool, light hand on her shoulder.

"It isn't as bad as that. Or it won't be, anyway—after you've told me about it."

She waited. Suddenly the woman in bed twisted about and sat up. Her breathing was quick.

"They've got away from me," she cried. Martha Foote had heard the rumors. She knew what Geisha McCoy meant. "I can't hold the audience anymore. In fact, the harder I work, the colder they get. And, oh, my God! Now they sit and *knit!*"

"Knit!" echoed Martha Foote. "But everybody's knitting nowadays."

"Not when *I'm* onstage! They can't! But they do. There were three of them in the third row yesterday afternoon. One of 'em was doing a sock. The second was doing a sweater, and the third a cap. I could tell by the shape. How can I sing my heart out? Not when I'm hypnotized by three stony-faced women doubled up over their knitting needles! And all their yarn is olive-drab—the color of uniforms! I'm scared of it. It sticks out all over the theater.

"Last night in the first row, there were two young kids in uniform. I'll bet the oldest of them wasn't even 23. There they sat, looking up at me with their baby faces. That's all they are—*kids*. The theater is full of them. I see olive drab day and night. I never seem to see anything else. I can't—"

Her head came down on her arms that

were already clasped around her knees.

"Somebody you love in the war?" Martha Foote asked, quietly. She waited. Then she made a wild guess. "Son?"

"How did you know?" Geisha McCoy's head shot up.

"I didn't. It was just a guess."

"Well, you're right. There aren't 50 people in the world who know I've got a grown-up son. It's bad for business to have them think you're middle-aged. Besides, my Fred doesn't care for the stage. He's an engineer. Third year at Boston Tech."

"Is he still there?"

"He's in France! Somewhere—in France. That's why I've worked for 22 years. Just for the time when that kid would step off on his own. I never went on without thinking of him. And now? I can't even hold him anymore. I'm through, I tell you. I'm *through*!"

Martha Foote dived right in. "It's up to you to turn things around. You can make those three women in the third row forget why they're knitting. That's your job. You're lucky to have a job like that."

"Lucky?"

"Yes, ma'am! You can do all that *dumka* stuff in private—the way Anna Czarnik does. But it's up to you to help your audience be happy twice a day."

"It's all very well for you to talk that cheerful stuff. The war hasn't come home to you, I can see that."

Martha Foote smiled. "I hope you don't mind my saying something, Miss McCoy. But you're too worn out from lack of sleep to see anything clearly. Why, a year ago, Anna Czarnic would have been the most interesting thing in this town to you. You'd have copied her clothes. You'd have learned her song. You'd have made her as real to your audiences as she was to us this morning. You'd have made people *feel* her tragic history. You'd have made them love her, and understand her. That's what's wrong with you, my dear. You're so wrapped up in your own troubles that you've lost your human touch. And that was just what your fans most loved about you!"

Geisha McCoy was looking up at Martha Foote with a half-smile. "Look here. You know too much. You're not really the hotel housekeeper, are you?"

"Indeed I am. I've been earning my living here ever since my husband died."

"Are you happy?"

"I must be—because I never stop to think about it. It's my job to know everything that concerns the comfort of the guests in this hotel."

"Including hysterics in 618?"

"Including."

Geisha McCoy settled down into the pillows. "I think I can sleep now,"she said. She took Martha Foote's hand between her own and squeezed it hard. "Thanks," she smiled. "Just turn out those lights, will you? And sort of tiptoe out." Then, as Martha Foote reached the door, she said, "Do you think old Anna would sell me her shoes?"

Martha Foote didn't get her dinner that night until almost eight. Still, as days go, it wasn't as bad as Monday. She and Irish Nellie, who had come in to turn down Martha Foote's bed, agreed on that. The Senate Hotel housekeeper was having her dinner in her room while Irish Nellie talked away.

"That lady in 618 kinda calmed down, didn't she? She sure had us jumping yesterday. Seems like some folks just don't have any feelings."

Martha Foote unfolded her napkin. "You can't always judge, Nellie. That woman's got a son who has gone to war. She can't see how to live without him. She's better now. I talked to her this evening at six. She said she had a fine afternoon."

"She's not the only one with troubles! And what do you hear from *your* boy, Miss Foote? Any word from France?"

"He's well—his arm's all healed. He says he'll be back in the fighting again any day."

"Humph," said Irish Nellie. She got ready to leave. Then she sniffed a familiar smell. "Well, for land sakes, Miss Foote! If I was housekeeper here, I wouldn't be eating that. I'd have me some strawberries, and fancy chicken, and ice cream, if I could. I wouldn't be eating plain old corned beef and cabbage for my dinner! Not me!"

"Oh, yes, you would, Nellie," replied Martha Foote, quietly. She spooned up some cabbage drippings. "Oh, yes, you would."

Shore Leave

What surprises are in store for a country boy who joins the navy? Tyler Kamps has never seen a city before—let alone a glamorous place like Chicago. Will his first shore leave be everything he expects it to be?

GUNNER MORAN HAD JAMMED A LIFETIME OF
ADVENTURE INTO HIS TEN YEARS AT SEA.

Shore Leave

Tyler Kamps was tired from the tips of his toes to the top of his head. He was as tired as only a fellow who has risen at 5:30 A.M. can be at 9:30 P.M. Yet he lay wide awake in his hammock, eight feet above the ground. Like a giant silkworm in a cocoon, he listened to the sleep-sounds around him. They came from two hundred other cocoons just like his.

A chorus of soft, regular breathing filled the long, dark room. An occasional grunt or sigh told of deeper sleep. Tyler Kamps should have been part of this chorus himself. Instead, he lay staring into the darkness. His mind was busy thinking mad thoughts.

"Gosh! Wouldn't I like to sit up in my hammock and give one yell!" he was thinking. "Like a movie cowboy gives on a Saturday night. Wake 'em up and stop that—darned old breathing."

Nerves. He tried to breathe deeply himself, once or twice. Somehow, it seemed to make him feel better. Then sleep claimed him at last. From his hammock, too, came the sound of deep, regular breathing. Once in a while there was a small grunt or soft sigh. Just the normal sleep-sounds of a very tired boy.

The trouble with Tyler Kamps was that he was homesick. He missed two things that he hadn't expected to miss at all. And he missed not at all the things he had expected to miss.

First of all, he had expected to miss his mother. If you knew Stella Kamps, you would have understood that. She was the kind of mother they write songs about—mother, pal, and sweetheart. That was where she had made her big mistake. Everybody knows what happens when a mother tries to be all those things to her son. That son has a good chance of turning out soft and spoiled. The war was probably what saved Tyler Kamps from becoming a mollycoddle.

Stella Kamps and her boy were different from other people, anyway. All the folks in Marvin, Texas, agreed about that. Flowers on the table at meals. Getting all worked up about things in books. Reading out loud to each other. Folks in Marvin knew how hard Stella Kamps worked to earn a living. They knew what a good housekeeper she was. They knew what a fight she had to put up after that good-for-nothing Kamps up and left her. If she spoiled her son, well— they could understand.

So Tyler had expected to miss her most of all. The way she talked, and the way she fussed around him without seeming to fuss. Her special way of cooking things. Her laugh, which made him laugh, and the funny way she had of saying things. She made ordinary things seem special.

And now he missed her only as any young man of 21 can miss his mother. No more and no less.

He had expected to miss his friends at the bank, and he had expected to miss the Mandolin Club. Every Thursday night, he and four other mandolin players had spangled the Texas night with their tinkling music.

He had expected to miss the familiar faces on Main Street. He had expected to miss the neighbors. All the little everyday things about life back home in Marvin, Texas, he had expected to miss.

And he didn't.

For ten weeks he had been at the Great Central Naval Training Station near Chicago, Illinois. And there were just two things he missed the most.

He wanted the quiet and privacy of his small bedroom back home. And he wanted to talk to a girl.

Tyler definitely knew that he wanted the first. He didn't know as yet that he wanted the second. The fact that he didn't know it was his mother's fault. Because she loved and needed him so much, she had kept girls away from him. She gave him all her attention. The girls back in Marvin, Texas, had given up on him. He seemed to be hopeless.

His room back home hadn't been much. It was bare and clean. There was a narrow, white bed and a maple dresser. In one corner was a bookshelf that he had made himself. Stella Kamps had filled the bookcase with good books. Before she married Clint Kamps, she had been a Kansas schoolteacher. And she had never quite got over it. But the books that Tyler liked best—the thumb-marked, grimy ones—were the adventure stories.

It was a hot little room in the Texas summers, and a cold little room in the Texas winters. But it was his own. And quiet. In the morning it had been pleasant to wake up there. Delicious breakfast smells would come up from the kitchen. His mother would call from the foot of the stairs, "*Ty*-ler! *Ty*-ler! Get up, son! Breakfast is on the table."

Before the Great Central Naval Training Station, Tyler had never been anywhere. The closest he had come to sea life was sailing wood chips in the wash tub. Marvin, Texas, is 500 miles inland. Yet he had enlisted in the navy without thinking twice. It was as if he came from a long line of sailors. His boyhood choice of games was always pirate. At 12, he could use big words like *mizzentopsail-yard* and *maintopgallant-mast*. He knew every part of a full-rigged ship—just from his pictures and books.

At 21, Tyler had finished business college. But he had never kissed a girl, or been in love. Right out of school, he went to work in the Texas State Savings Bank. Sometimes girls would come inside just to look at his handsome face. One girl kept coming in to get nickels changed to a dollar. Then she came back again for nickels. No doubt her visits would have gone on and on. But then Tyler's country had given him something more important to do.

On the day Tyler left for the naval training station, his mother did not whimper. She showed the stuff she was made of. Down at the train, she smiled up at him and told him goodbye. His blond head was only one of many thrust out the open windows.

". . . and Tyler, remember to keep your feet dry. I'll send a box every week. Don't eat too many of the nut cookies. Won't it be grand to be right there on the water! You'll write once a week, won't you, dear? . . . You're—you're moving. The train's going! Good-b—"

She ran alongside the train for a few feet. Then suddenly, with a great pang, she thought: "Oh, my God, how young he is! And he doesn't know anything. I should have told him . . . things. . . . He doesn't know anything about—"

She ran on, as if running could hold onto him a moment longer. "Tyler!" she called, through the noise and shouting. "Tyler, be good! Be good!" He could only see her lips moving, but he nodded his head. Then he waved one last time.

So Tyler Kamps had traveled up to Chicago. He, who had never been more than a two-hours ride from home, was out in the real world.

The first few days there had been unbelievably bad. There were typhoid shots, smallpox vaccinations, and shocking loneliness. Most of the other guys in his barracks were older and more experienced. Seeing his pink cheeks and blond hair, they gave him the nickname Sweetheart. The name stuck.

Tyler felt bewildered and unhappy. He wondered where the *sea* part of the training came in. Learning to sleep in a hammock took him a week.

Then Tyler met Gunner Moran. He had hairy, tattooed arms and bright blue eyes. In fact, Gunner Moran wasn't a gunner at all. He was just a seaman who knew the sea from China to Spain. He knew knots and sails and rifles and bayonets. Just barely 25, he already had ten years of sea experience. Into those ten years he had jammed a lifetime of adventure. He could do well at all the things that Tyler Kamps did poorly.

In Tyler's barracks, Gunner Moran was company commander. In rank, he was only a lowly "gob," like all the other 200 of them. But in power and influence he was a captain.

Moran taught his men how to thrust with the bayonet. He taught them to shoot. He could box like a professional. Tyler adored him. This was partly because he was fatherless. Tyler couldn't remember a time when there was a big man around who could eat more or throw farther than he could.

In Tyler's third week at the naval station, several young sailors came down with mumps. His barracks was quarantined. This meant that no one could leave. Tyler did not catch the mumps, but he had to endure the weeks of being shut in.

At first everybody took it as a lark. Moran's hammock was just next to Tyler's. On the other side was a young Kentuckian named Dabney Courtney. The barracks called him *Monicker*.

Monicker had a beautiful tenor voice. Moran had a salty bass. And Tyler had his mandolin. All of them sang a great deal. They bawled every song they knew. They read. They talked. And they grew sick of the sight of one another.

Sometimes they gathered around Moran. He told them tales they only half believed. He had been in the far-off places that boys only read about in travel books. Moran showed them the tattoos on his arms and chest. There were anchors, and serpents, and hearts with arrows stuck through them. Each mark had its story. Moran had an easy way about him. His stories made the sailors feel that they knew very little of life.

Visiting day was the worst. The whole group of them grew savage, somehow. It was hard to watch the mothers and sisters and cousins and sweethearts stream by. All of them were going to the other barracks. A sailor Tyler didn't know suddenly showed him a picture of his girlfriend. She was a healthy, wide-awake looking, small-town girl.

"She's vice-president of the Silver Star Pleasure Club back home. I'm president," the boy told Tyler. "We meet every other Saturday." Tyler looked at the picture approvingly. Suddenly he wished that he had a picture of such a girl. He took out his mother's picture and showed it.

"Oh, yeah," said the boy, with no interest at all.

The dragging weeks of quarantine came to an end. At the end of the week, they were to be given shore leave. Tyler had decided to go to Chicago. He had never been there before.

Five-thirty. Reveille.

Tyler awoke with the feeling that something was going to happen. Something very pleasant. Then he remembered, and smiled.

Tyler had no pal. His years of closeness to his mother had left him somewhat shy. He heard the other boys talking. They were making plans for shore leave. Chicago was their goal. Six weeks of stored-up energy had made them all as wild as young colts in the spring.

"Going to Chicago, kid?" Moran asked him. It was Saturday morning.

"Yes. Are you?"

"You bet."

At the Y.M.C.A. they had given him free tickets for some city entertainments. They told him about free clubs. They gave him the names of places where a fellow could get a good meal, cheap.

One of the tickets was for a dance. Tyler knew nothing of dancing. This dance was to be given at some kind of women's club. He *did* know that a dance meant he could meet some girls. Why hadn't he ever learned to dance?

Tyler walked down to the station and waited for the train. It would bring him to Chicago about one o'clock. The other boys stood in little groups, or in pairs. They were smoking and talking. Tyler wanted to join them, but he held back. They all seemed to know just what they were doing as they made their plans. They knew all about places to go, and amusements, and girls. On the train, they all bought candy. They stuffed down chocolate as greedily as children.

Tyler found himself in the same car with Moran. He edged over to a seat near him and watched him closely. Moran was not mingling with the other boys. He kept apart, his sea-blue eyes gazing out at the flat Illinois prairie. All through the car there was excited talk.

"They say there's a swell supper in the Tower Building for fifty cents."

"Fifty nothing. Get all you want at the library canteen for nothing."

"Where's this dance, huh?"

"Search *me*."

"Hey, Murph! I'll shoot you a game of pool at the club."

"Naw, I gotta date."

Tyler's eyes met Moran's. Moran's upper lip curled up in disgust. "Navy! This ain't no navy no more. It's a Sunday school, that's what! All this talk about phonographs, and church suppers, and dances! It's enough to turn a fella's stomach. Lot of Sunday school kids who don't know a sail from a tablecloth."

Moran fell into scornful silence.

A moment before, Tyler had felt jealous of the other boys. He had envied their knowledge of these very things. Now he smiled at Moran. "That's right," he said. Moran looked at him for a moment, curiously. Then he went back to staring out the window.

In Moran's head there was as much bewilderment as there was in Tyler's. But Moran's confusion was for a much different reason. Gunner Moran was of the *old* navy. His navy had been despised and spat upon. His uniform alone had kept him out of decent places. It kept him from contact with decent people. It had pushed him into saloons, and shooting galleries, and low-down dives.

Now, to Moran's confusion, the public had done an about-face. Suddenly its doors were open to him. Now society had closed its saloons to him and invited him home. It sat him down at its table, and introduced him to its daughter.

"Nothing doing!" said Gunner Moran, and spat between his teeth. "Not for me. I pick my own lady friends."

Gunner Moran was used to picking his own lady friends. He had picked them all over the world.

At last the train drew in at the great Northwestern station. In a flash, Gunner Moran was out and gone. He was down the steps and up the long platform before the wheels stopped turning.

Tyler came down the steps slowly. A flood of blue uniforms streamed past him. The sailors' white or blue caps flowed like waves to the great doorway. Then they were gone.

In Tyler's town, back home in Marvin, Texas, people knew the trains by number. There was Number 11 and Number 55. Everybody knew their schedules, too. "I reckon Number 55'll be late today. On account of the storm," people would say.

Now he saw half a dozen trains lined up at once. A dozen more tracks waited, empty. The great train station awed him. The huge waiting room was full of hurrying people. Tyler felt lost and alone. He stood, a rather dazed blue figure, in the vastness of that shining place.

A kindly Red Cap saved him. He knew a lost young sailor when he saw one. And he had seen many! "Jackies" is what they called these new, young seamen.

The Red Cap led Tyler through the great building to the sailors' club rooms. He showed him the tubs for scrubbing clothes and the steam dryers. He showed Tyler the bathtubs and the lunch room. "Could I clean up here? And wash my things? Could I take a bath in a bathtub, with all the hot water I want?" Tyler asked his guide.

"You sure can. Just wait around and grab your turn."

Tyler waited. And he watched to see how the other boys did things. He read, listened to the phonograph, and watched. Finally, his turn came, and he seized it.

Tyler's ceremony of cleanliness would have made his mother proud. All her years of pointing him toward soap and water were now paying off.

First Tyler scrubbed out a tub. Then he scalded the brush and scrubbed the tub again. Then he took off all his clothes and scrubbed everything. He scrubbed and rinsed and flapped. Finally he hung all his clothes neatly—from trousers to cap—in the dryers. Then, with a deep sigh of accomplishment, he took a bath. He splashed in the hot water until the boys who were waiting threatened to pull him out. Then he wrapped up in a sheet. He lay down on one of the green velvet couches and fell fast asleep.

An hour later Tyler woke up. His clothes were neatly folded. It seemed that another sailor had wanted to use his drying space.

Tyler put his clean clothes on. He stood before a mirror and brushed his hair until it glittered. Clean and dressed, he sailed forth onto the streets of Chicago, in search of adventure.

He soon found it.

Trying not to show how nervous he felt in the roaring city, he strode along. On the surface, he was a carefree sailor on shore leave. Beneath, he was a forlorn and lonely Texas boy.

It was late afternoon. The spring day

had been mild, but now there was a snap in the evening air. Tyler felt restless. He wished he had someone to talk to. He thought of the man on the train who had said, "I got a date." Tyler wished that he, too, had a date.

For a moment he stood on a bridge. Then he went on, looking about with big eyes. When he compared Chicago, Illinois, with Marvin, Texas, he found Chicago sadly lacking. The noise and rush tired him out. Soon he came to a moving picture theater. He saw a pretty girl sitting in the ticket booth. Tyler walked up to the window and shoved his money through the little opening. The girl fed him a ticket without looking up. "How long does the show take?" he asked. He wanted her to talk to him.

" 'Bout an hour," said the girl, meeting his eyes.

"Thanks," said Tyler, with a big smile. But no answering smile curved the lady's lips. Tyler went in. A so-called comedy was playing, but Tyler was not amused. It was followed by a war picture. Tyler

left before the show was over. He was
very hungry by now. A dairy lunch room
seemed to invite him. He liked its white
tiles, and pans of baked apples, and
browned beans. He went in and ate a
solitary supper, heavy on pie and cake.

When he came out to the street again,
it was dark. Walking over to State Street,
he took the dance card out of his pocket
and looked at it again. If only he had
learned to dance! There'd *have* to be girls
at a dance.

Suddenly, he heard a woman's voice,
very soft and low. "Hello, Sweetheart!"
the voice said. His nickname! He whirled
around eagerly.

The girl was a stranger to him. But she
was smiling, and she was pretty—sort of.
"Hello, Sweetheart!" she said again.

"Why, how-do, ma'am," said Tyler, in
his best Texas style.

"Where you going, kid?" she asked.

Tyler blushed a little. "Well, nowhere
in particular, ma'am."

"Come on along with me then," she
said. She linked her arm in his.

"Why—why—thanks, but—"

Tyler could hardly believe it. Texas people were always saying that easterners weren't friendly! He felt a little uneasy, though, as he looked down into her smiling face. There was something—

"Hello, Sweetheart!" said another voice. It was a man's voice this time. Out of a cigar store stepped Gunner Moran. A strange feeling of relief and gladness swept over Tyler. And then Moran looked sharply at the girl. "Why, hello, Blanche!" he said.

"Hello yourself," the girl answered. Now her face had a sour look.

"Thought you was in 'Frisco," Gunner said.

"Well, I ain't."

"Friend of yours?" Moran asked Tyler.

Before Tyler could open his mouth, the girl said, "Sure he is. Sure I am. We been around together all afternoon."

Tyler jerked away. "Why, ma'am, I guess you've made a mistake! I never saw you before in my life."

The smile faded from the girl's face. Now her forehead wrinkled in fury. She glared at Moran. "Who are you to go butting into my business! This guy's a friend of mine, I tell ya!"

"Yeah? Well, he's a friend of mine, too. Me and him had a date to meet right here. We're going over to a swell little dance on Michigan Avenue. So it's *you* who's butting in, Blanche, me girl."

The young woman stood twisting her handkerchief angrily. "I'll get you for this!" she hissed.

"Beat it!" said Moran. He tucked his arm through Tyler's and started walking briskly up the street. The girl stared after them.

Tyler Kamps was an innocent—but he was not a fool. He realized that he had been rescued. Now there seemed to be a strong, new bond between him and Moran. Tyler thought it must be like the feeling between a father and son who understand each other.

Man-like, they did not talk about what they were thinking.

Tyler broke the silence.

"Do you dance?"

"Me! Dance! Well, I ain't what you'd rightly call a real good dancer. Why are you asking?"

"Because I can't dance, either. But let's just go up and see what it's like, anyway."

"See what *what's* like?"

"This dance we're going to."

They had reached the address printed on the card. Tyler stopped to look up at the great, brightly lighted building. Moran stopped too, but for a different reason. He was staring in open-mouthed surprise at Tyler Kamps.

"You mean to say that you thought I was going—" he choked. "Oh, my God!"

Tyler smiled. "I'm kind of scared, too. But Monicker goes to these dances, and he says they're nice. Lots of pretty girls. *Nice* girls. I wouldn't go alone. But you— you're used to dancing and—girls."

Tyler linked his arm through the other man's. In a daze, Moran allowed himself to be moved along. Quickly he found himself in an elevator with a dozen red-cheeked, scrubbed-looking sailors.

The elevator stopped at the ninth floor. "Out here for the jackies' dance," said the elevator boy.

Tyler and Moran stepped out with the others. The hall was full of women and girls. Talk. Laughter. In another minute the terrified pair would have turned and fled. But in that tiny half-moment of hesitation, they were lost.

A woman came toward them, hand outstretched. She was tall, slim, and friendly looking. She wore a silk gown.

"Good evening!" she said. It was as if she had been waiting for them all evening. "I'm so glad to see you. You can check your caps right here. Do you dance?"

Two scarlet faces. Four hands twisting at white caps. "Why, no, ma'am."

"That's fine. We'll teach you. Then you can go into the ballroom and have a wonderful time."

"But—" began Moran.

"Oh, Miss Hall! Over here!" She called to a tiny blonde in blue. "Miss Hall, this

is Mr.—ah—Mr. Moran. And Mr.?—yes—
Mr. Kamps. Tyler Kamps. They want to
learn to dance. I'll turn them right over
to you. When does your class begin?"

Miss Hall glanced at her watch.
"Starting right now," she said, crisply.
She looked at the two men. "I'm sure
you'll both make wonderful dancers.
Follow me."

She turned. The two men stared at her
back and then at each other. Flight was
in the mind of both. Then Miss Hall
turned and smiled. She held out a small
hand. "Come on," she said. "Follow me."

As though hypnotized, Tyler and
Moran followed her.

She led them into a large room, with a
piano in one corner. Groups of fidgeting
sailors stood in every other corner. At the
sight of them, Moran and Tyler sighed
with relief. At least they were not to be
alone in their misery.

Miss Hall wasted no time. Head held
high, she stood in the center of the room.
"Now then, form a circle, please!"

At those words, 20 healthy examples

of young manhood suddenly became shambling hulks. They clumped forward, breathing hard. "A little lively, please. Don't hold back. Now then, Miss Weeks! A fox trot."

Miss Weeks was at the piano. She broke into a spirited tune. The first stumbling steps in the social career of Gunner Moran and Tyler Kamps had begun.

Miss Hall was strictly business. No nonsense about her. "One-two-three-four! And a *one*-two *three*-four. One-two-three-four! And a *turn*-two, *turn* four. Now then, all together. Just four straight steps as if you were walking down the street. That's it! One-two-three-four! Don't look at me—look at my feet. And a *one*-two-*three*-four!"

Red faced, they were. Very earnest. Pathetically eager. Weeks of drilling had taught them to obey commands. To them, the little dancing teacher was more than just a pretty girl. She was knowledge. She was power. She was the commanding officer. Like children, they obeyed her.

Tyler had what is known as a "rhythm sense." An expert whistler is usually a natural dancer. Tyler was such a whistler. And his dancing was much like his whistling.

Tyler was never a half-beat behind the tireless Miss Weeks. Little Miss Hall had a skilled eye for talent. She picked him out at once.

"You've danced before?"

"No, ma'am."

"Take the head of the line, please. Now, all of you—watch Mr. Kamps! Then, all together, please."

And they were off again. At 9:45 Tyler Kamps and Gunner Moran were standing in the crowded doorway of the ballroom. They were in a panic. What if some girl should ask them to dance? What if *no* girl asked them? Little Miss Hall had brought them right up to the door. She had left them there with stern orders not to move. Then she had dashed off to find them partners.

"Let's duck," Moran whispered. The band crashed into the opening bars of a lively fox trot.

"Oh, it wouldn't seem—" But it was plain that Tyler was weakening. They were about to turn and run when they saw little Miss Hall coming their way. Her blonde head bobbed in and out among the dancing couples. She had one girl on her right and another one on her left. The force of her bright eyes held her two victims in the doorway. They watched her approach. Now they were helpless.

A soft groan escaped Moran's lips. Miss Hall and the two girls stood before them, cool and smiling.

"Miss Cunningham, this is Mr. Tyler Kamps. Mr. Moran, Miss Cunningham. Miss Drew—Mr. Moran, Mr. Kamps."

The two sailors gulped, bowed, and mumbled something.

"Would you like to dance?" said Miss Cunningham. She raised her eyes to Tyler's.

"Why—I—you see, I don't really know how. I just started to—"

"Oh, *that's* quite all right," Miss

Cunningham said, cheerfully. "We'll try it." In a daze, Tyler found himself moving across the floor in time to the music. He didn't know that he was being led, but he was. She didn't try to talk and he breathed a prayer of thanks for that. Somehow she seemed to know about those four straight steps, then two to the right and two to the left. Then four again. And turn-two, turn-four.

Tyler didn't know that he was desperately counting aloud. Just then he didn't even know that this was a *girl* he was dancing with. He seemed to move automatically. Afterwards, he was never quite clear about those first ten minutes of his ballroom experience.

The music stopped. There was applause. Tyler mopped his head and his hands. He applauded too, like a man in a movie. Then they were off again.

Five minutes later he found himself seated next to Miss Cunningham. They were in chairs against the wall. The mists of agony cleared from his gaze. For the first time he saw Miss Cunningham

herself. She was a tall, slim, dark-haired
girl. There was a glint of mischief in her
eye. She looked as if she were trying to
keep from smiling.

"Why don't you?" Tyler asked. Then he
was horrified at himself.

"Why don't I what?"

"Smile, if you want to."

She laughed. Tyler laughed, too. Then
they laughed together and were friends.

"Where are you from?"

"Why, I'm from Texas, ma'am. Marvin,
Texas."

"Is that so? So many of the boys are
from Texas. Are you out at the station or
on one of the boats?"

"I'm on the station. Yes, ma'am."

"Do you like the navy?"

"Yes, ma'am, I do. I sure do. You know
there isn't a drafted man in the navy. No,
ma'am. We're all enlisted men."

"When do you think the war will end,
Mr. Kamps?"

He told her what he thought. Then he
told her many other things. He told her
about Texas. Like all Texans, he went on

and on about the size of the state. "Why, Big Y Ranch alone would make the whole country of Germany look like a cattle grazing patch. It's bigger than all those countries in Europe strung together. And every man in Texas would rather fight than eat. Yes, ma'am. Why, you couldn't hold 'em back."

"My!" breathed Miss Cunningham.

They danced again. Miss Cunningham introduced him to some other girls, and he danced with them. They also asked him about the naval station, and about Texas. Tyler had such a beautiful time that he completely forgot about Gunner Moran. It was not until he and Miss Cunningham went downstairs for refreshments that he remembered his friend. He had gotten hot chocolate for himself and Miss Cunningham. Also sandwiches, and chunks of delicious caramel cake. They were talking, and eating, and enjoying themselves. Tyler had gone back for more cake at the white-clothed table, when he suddenly remembered. A look of horror came over his face. He gasped.

"W-what's the matter?" demanded Miss Cunningham.

"My—my friend, Gunner Moran. I forgot all about him!"

"Oh, that's quite all right," Miss Cunningham told him for the second time that evening. "We'll just go and find him. He's probably forgotten all about you, too."

And for the second time she was right. Their search was a short one. In the next room, there were many groups of sailors and girls. All were talking, and laughing, and eating huge quantities of cake. In the center of one group sat Gunner Moran. He held a large square of chocolate cake in one hand. His little finger was crooked elegantly over a cup in his other hand. Four very pretty girls surrounded him.

As Tyler and Miss Cunningham came near, they could hear him talking. "Yes, sir!" he was saying. "It's got so I can't sleep in anything *but* a hammock. Why, when I was just 17 years old I was—" He caught Tyler's eye. "Hello!" he called. "Meet my friend," he said to the ladies around him. "I was just telling these ladies here—"

And he was off again. Some of the tales he told were not exactly true. But his audience grew larger as he talked. And he talked and talked. Finally, he and Tyler had to run all the way to the station for the last train. When he left the ballroom, Moran shook hands like a presidential candidate.

"I never met a finer bunch of ladies," he told them. "Sure I'm coming back again. Ask me! I've had an elegant time. Simply *elegant*."

He and Tyler did not talk much on the train. It was a sleepy lot of sailors that were carried back to the Great Central Naval Station. Tyler was undressed and in his hammock even before Moran.

Quiet fell over the great, dim barracks. Tyler felt himself slipping off to sleep. She would be there next Saturday. Her first name was Myrtle—just about the prettiest name he had ever heard. Her folks invited sailors to dinner nearly every Sunday. Maybe, if they gave him 36 hours of leave next time—

"Hey, Sweetheart!" It was a hissing whisper from Moran's hammock.

"What?"

"Say, was that four steps and then turn-turn? Or four and two steps to the side? I kinda forgot."

"Oh, shut up!" growled Monicker. "Let a fellow sleep, can't you! What do you think this is, a boarding school?"

"Shut up, yourself!" answered Tyler, happily. "It's four steps. Then two to the right and two to the left. Then four again. Then turn two, turn two.

"Oh, yeah. I was pretty sure," said Moran, humbly.

Quiet settled down in the huge room. Soon there were only the sounds of deep, regular breathing. Once in a while, there was a grunt or a sigh. The normal sleep sounds of very tired young sailors.

꧁꧂

Thinking About
the Stories

Representing T.A. Buck

1. Can you think of any other good titles for this story?

2. Compare and contrast two characters in this story. In what ways are they alike? In what ways are they different?

3. Does the main character in this story have an internal conflict? Does a terrible decision have to be made? Explain the character's choices.

The Three of Them

1. Many stories are meant to teach a lesson of some kind. Is the author trying to make a point in this story? What is it?

2. Suppose that this story was the first chapter in a book of many chapters. What would happen next?

3. Which character in this story do you most admire? Why? Which character do you like the least?

Shore Leave

1. How important is the background of the story? Is weather a factor in the story? Is there a war going on or some other unusual circumstance? What influence does the background have on the characters' lives?

2. Interesting story plots often have unexpected twists and turns. What surprises did you find in this story?

3. Who is the main character in this story? Who are one or two of the minor characters? Describe each of these characters in one or two sentences.